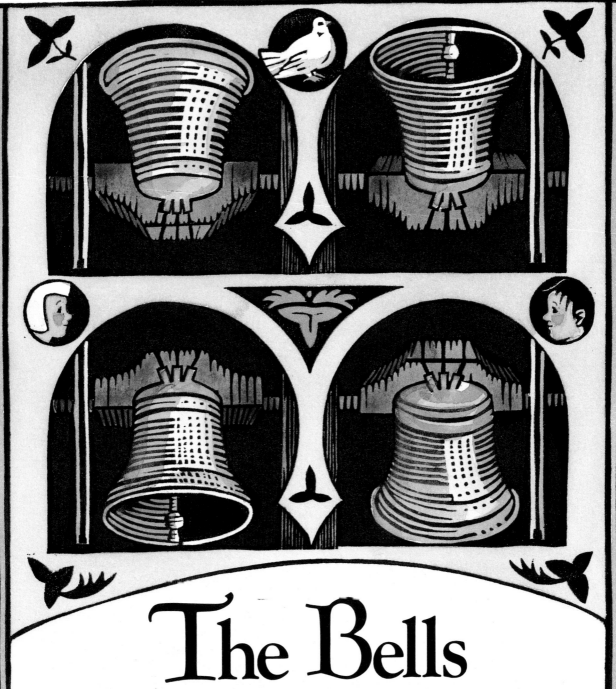

The Bells of London

with a story in pictures by
ASHLEY WOLFF

Dodd, Mead & Company • New York

For Sabin

Distributed in Canada by
McClelland and Stewart Limited, Toronto
Printed in Hong Kong by South China Printing Company
1 2 3 4 5 6 7 8 9 10
Library of Congress Cataloging in Publication Data
Wolff, Ashley.   The bells of London.
Summary: Illustrations depicting the activities of a
variety of long-ago Londoners accompany the traditional
rhyme about the many church bells of the city.
1. Nursery rhymes.   2. Children's poetry, English. [1. Nursery
rhymes.   2. Churches—Poetry.   3. London—Poetry]   I. Title.
PZ8.3.W843Be 1985   398'.8   84-13787
ISBN 0-396-08485-0

"The Bells of London"
is a fine old ditty,
naming churches of
England's capital city.
Look down in the streets
as the bells ring above,
see the tale of a girl,
a boy, and a dove.

Gay go up and gay go down, to ring the bells of London Town:

Oranges and lemons,
say the bells of
St. Clement's.

Pancakes and fritters,
say the bells of
St. Peter's.

Brickbats and tiles,
say the bells of
St. Giles'.

Two sticks and an apple,
say the bells of
Whitechapel.

Bull's-eyes and targets,
say the bells of
St. Margaret's.

Old Father Baldpate,
say the slow bells of
Aldgate.

Maids in white aprons,
say the bells of
St. Catherine's.

Poker and tongs,
say the bells of
St. John's.

Kettles and pans,
say the bells of
St. Anne's.

You owe me five farthings,
say the bells of
St. Martin's.

When will you pay me?
say the bells of
Old Bailey.

When I grow rich,
say the bells of
Shoreditch.

Pray, when will that be?
say the bells of Stepney.